Copyright © 2004 by Edition Jürgen Lassig,
an imprint of Nord-Süd Verlag AG, Gossau Zürich, Switzerland
First published in Switzerland under the title *Toddels tollster Freund*.
English translation copyright © 2004 by North-South Books Inc., New York
All rights reserved. No part of this book may be reproduced or utilized in any form
or by any means, electronic or mechanical, including photocopying, recording, or any
information storage and retrieval system, without permission in writing from the publisher.

First published in the United States, Great Britain, Canada, Australia, and New Zealand in 2004
by North-South Books, an imprint of Nord-Süd Verlag AG, Gossau Zürich, Switzerland.
Distributed in the United States by North-South Books Inc., New York.

Library of Congress Cataloging-in-Publication Data is available.
A CIP catalogue record for this book is available from The British Library.
ISBN 0-7358-1920-3 (trade edition)
1 3 5 7 9 HC 10 8 6 4 2
ISBN 0-7358-1921-1 (library edition)
1 3 5 7 9 LE 10 8 6 4 2
Printed in Belgium

For more information about our books,
and the authors and artists who create them,
visit our web site: www.northsouth.com

There stood a bear cub.

"Hello, I'm Bruno," said the bear. "Can I play with you?"

Timmy and Rocket had never played with a bear before. Only with hares.

But Bruno seemed quite friendly.

"Okay," said Timmy.

Bruno was very strong. He could throw the ball even higher than Rocket—so high that they could hardly see it.

"Wow!" said Timmy. "That's great!"

It wasn't so great when the ball got stuck in the branches of a big oak tree.

"How are we going to get it down?" asked Rocket.

Bruno had an idea.

Rocket climbed onto Bruno and Timmy climbed onto Rocket. Then with a long stick Timmy reached for the ball. He almost had it, when—*thump!*—down he fell.

"Are you hurt?" asked Bruno.

Of course he was hurt—and his ball was still stuck in the tree.

Bruno had another idea. He showed Timmy and Rocket how to build a seesaw.

"You two stand on that end," said Bruno. "When I jump onto the other end, your side will go up and you can easily grab the ball."

So Timmy and Rocket got onto the seesaw and Bruno climbed onto a rocky ledge and jumped.

Timmy and Rocket were flung high. They did manage to knock down the ball as they sailed through the air, but they landed in the middle of a prickly bramble bush. "Ow! Ow!" they cried.

"Oh, I'm sorry. I'm so sorry!" said Bruno. He rushed to help Timmy and Rocket, but stumbled and fell—right on top of the wonderful new ball.

The ball was ruined—squashed flat, and Timmy
was really angry.

"You . . . you . . . you bear you!" he shouted at
Bruno. "Look what you've done!"

"I didn't mean to do it," said Bruno sadly.

Timmy didn't care. "I don't want to play with you
ever again!" he declared.

Furiously, he hopped home.

"Where is your new ball?" asked Timmy's mother.

"It's broken," said Timmy. "But I didn't do it—Bruno did." He told his mother all about Bruno the bear. "I'll never play with him again."

"Just because he accidentally broke your ball?" asked Mother.

"Yes . . . no . . ." Timmy thought about it. "It's because he's a bear," he said finally, "not a hare like Rocket and me."

Mother just shook her head.

The next afternoon Timmy was waiting
for Rocket by the pond.
Timmy waited and waited. . . .

Suddenly Freddy the sly fox crept out of the woods.
"Well, who do we have here?" he asked, chuckling.
Timmy was petrified. Freddy was always looking for
trouble. He loved to torment little hares like Timmy.

"First I think I'll pull your ears and tie them in a knot. And then . . ." Freddie grinned. "Then I'll throw you into the pond!" He reached for Timmy's ears when suddenly . . .

. . . Bruno grabbed him. "Leave my friend alone!" Bruno roared and chased the frightened Freddy into the woods.

"Thanks, Bruno," said Timmy. "You were great!"

Bruno grinned. "It's no trouble at all for a bear cub," he said modestly.

"I'm glad you are a bear—a strong, brave bear—and not a little hare like me or Rocket," said Timmy, smiling.

Bruno had brought along a brand-new ball for Timmy.

So the three friends played happily together until the sun disappeared behind the treetops.